the Swan™ princess

Adapted by Francine Hughes
Based on a screenplay by Brian Nissen
From a story by Richard Rich and Brian Nissen

SCHOLASTIC INC.
New York   Toronto   London   Auckland   Sydney

No part of this publication may be reproduced in whole or in part, or stored in a retrieval system, or transmitted in any form, or by any means, electronic, mechanical, photocopying, recording, or otherwise, without written permission of the publisher. For information regarding permission, write to Nest Productions, Inc., 333 North Glenoaks Boulevard, Suite 400, Burbank, CA 91502.

ISBN 0-590-22203-1

Copyright © 1994 by Nest Productions, Inc.
All rights reserved. Published by Scholastic Inc., 555 Broadway, New York, NY 10012, by arrangement with Nest Productions, Inc.

12 11 10 9 8 7 6 5 4 3 2 1   4 5 6 7 8 9/9

Printed in the U.S.A.   24

First Scholastic printing, November 1994

Once upon a time, in a large and mighty kingdom, the Princess Odette was born. Kings and queens came from all around to offer gifts to the newborn princess. Queen Uberta brought her young son, Prince Derek. And as Derek gave Odette his gift — a pretty locket — their parents had a wonderful idea. Odette's father, King William, and Derek's mother, Queen Uberta, would bring the children together every summer. Maybe . . . just maybe . . . the two would fall in love, marry, and unite the two kingdoms.

3

But the evil enchanter Rothbart had a different plan. He wanted King William's kingdom — all for himself.

Back in his hideout, Rothbart gazed into his magical fires. "The kingdom will belong to me and me alone," he vowed.

Rothbart was soon banished from the kingdom for plotting against the king. But he remained determined. He would leave quietly with his assistant, an old ugly hag. But he would have his way — one day.

Years passed. Rothbart was forgotten. And each summer, Princess Odette and Prince Derek were brought together by their parents. At first, these visits didn't go as smoothly as the king and queen had wished. Neither child seemed to like the other and the two refused to play together. King William and Queen Uberta were ready to give up hope that the prince and princess would ever marry.

5

Then one fine summer day, Derek took Odette into his arms.

"Arrange the marriage!" he cried. "Odette is so beautiful."

"Thank you," said Odette. "But is beauty all that matters to you?"

"What else is there?" Derek asked, confused. He couldn't put his true feelings into words. And Odette was hurt. Didn't he care about *her*? The marriage was not to be.

6

Feeling sad, King William and Odette rode off into the forest. They were deep inside the woods when a figure appeared before them. It was Rothbart! At first, he seemed to be an ordinary man. But then there was a burst of light, and Rothbart was transformed into a great animal. The animal took flight, soaring high above the king and princess. An instant later, down he swooped—straight toward Odette!

News of the attack spread through the kingdoms. Odette was gone! She had disappeared without a trace! And all because of a fearsome great animal. An animal that was not what it seemed.

"My poor Odette," Derek said softly. "What has happened to you?"

Derek cried out in fear and loss. "Odette!" His voice broke the stillness of the woods, carrying deep into the darkness until it finally reached Swan Lake. But by then, it was just a whisper.

A sad-looking swan swimming on Swan Lake heard a rustling noise and lifted her head. Was someone calling her? No, it was only Rothbart coming toward her.

"See here, Odette," Rothbart told the swan. "You are under a spell. But it doesn't last the whole day. You will change back to human form as soon as the moon comes up. . . ."

9

Just then, a beam of moonlight touched the swan's wing. Suddenly Odette was no longer a swan. She was a beautiful princess once again, standing ankledeep in the water.

"The spell will be broken if you marry me," Rothbart explained. "That way I will become king. Or there is one other way. You can find someone who will declare everlasting love, and prove it to the world." Rothbart gave a nasty laugh. "But that seems unlikely since you can't leave Swan Lake for long. You will turn back into a swan when the moonlight leaves the lake . . . no matter where you are."

Odette did not run away. There was nowhere she could go. Instead, she made friends with Jean-Bob and Speed, a frog and a turtle who lived on the lake. Days and nights came and went, each one the same as before. But then Odette met a tough-talking bird named Puffin. And together, she and Puffin formed a plan to break the spell.

"We'll find Derek," he told the others, "and lure him back to the lake just when the moon is coming up. He'll see Odette change into a princess. He'll declare his love. And everyone will live happily ever after!"

At that very same moment, Derek was readying himself for battle with the great animal.

"Odette is alive," Derek told his friend, Bromley, turning his back on him. "No one else thinks so. But I do. And I'm going to rescue her."

Bromley swallowed nervously. It was time for Catch and Fire — archery practice at its most dangerous.

"Oh please, oh please, oh please," said Bromley as their teacher placed an apple on Bromley's head. Then Bromley raised his bow and arrow. Still muttering, he aimed his arrow at Derek's heart.

The arrow sliced through the air. Quickly, Derek spun around, catching the arrow right before contact. Then, with lightning speed, he sent it back toward Bromley. *Pffft*! It neatly sliced the apple in half. Derek was ready.

But first, Prince Derek had to puzzle out one thing: What was the great animal? Derek hurried to the royal library. He leafed through book after book, searching for an answer. "It's not what it seems," he said again and again. "What does that mean?" Finally he shouted, "Of course! That's it!"

He was just about to race off to the forest, when his mother came into the room. "Remember the great ball is tomorrow night," she told Derek.

"I'll be back in time," he promised. To himself he added, "after I find Odette!"

13

Odette and Puffin were already scouring the forest for Derek, as he and Bromley started their search.

"We are looking for an animal that can change its shape," Derek said to Bromley. "A harmless creature that approaches, and suddenly . . ."

Bromley eyed a dragonfly. "You mean it could be anything?"

Derek nodded and moved on. But Bromley was walking in another direction, following the dragonfly.

"Remember, it will look harmless," Derek muttered as he cleared a path. He moved a branch out of the way, and found himself face-to-face with Odette the swan.

"A swan?" said Derek, thinking Odette was the great animal. "Of course!"

He raised his bow and arrow. Odette gasped, and took off in flight. Prince Derek was below, giving chase.

"Our plan is working!" Puffin cried, joining Odette. "We'll lead him back to the lake!"

Odette beat her wings furiously. "He thinks I'm the enchanter! This is too dangerous!" But she had to keep going. It was the only way.

The sun was setting behind Odette and Puffin as they darted in and out of the forest. They soared high in the sky, then low to the ground. They kept one step ahead of the prince, but they were careful not to let him fall far behind.

16

At last, Odette and Puffin reached Swan Lake. Prince Derek came into the clearing a second later. Huffing and puffing, he paused for a moment, looking around. There was Rothbart's castle with a water dungeon below it. And there was the beautiful swan, floating on the water's edge.

Once again, Derek raised his bow and arrow. He took aim . . .

Suddenly, a ray of moonlight stretched across the lake. Then a sparkling light swirled and twinkled around the swan. Derek watched in awe as the beautiful swan turned into Princess Odette. Amazed, Derek dropped his bow on the ground.

"Hello, Derek," Odette said quietly, and they fell into each other's arms.

"I knew you were alive, Odette," Derek said. "I knew it!"

In the distance, Odette heard the heavy thud of Rothbart's footsteps.

"You can't stay," she told Derek. Quickly, she explained about Rothbart and his evil spell.

"Don't worry," Derek said. "I'll make a vow of everlasting love. And I'll do it at the ball tomorrow night to prove it to the world."

"Od-ette!" Rothbart was calling to her now. He was nearing the lake.

"Yes, tomorrow night," said Odette, pushing Derek back into the forest. "Now go!"

Reluctantly, the prince left his love behind, just as Rothbart crashed into the clearing.

Odette sighed. Derek had escaped just in time. They were safe. But then Rothbart held out the prince's bow; the one he had just dropped.

"Come to the ball! I will make a vow of everlasting love," he sneered, imitating Derek. "Ha!"

Rothbart hurled the bow into the lake. "I have news for you, Odette. You won't be able to attend the ball after all."

Odette looked at him fearlessly. "You can't stop me!" she cried.

"I won't have to," Rothbart answered. "You see, tomorrow night . . . there is no moon!"

Laughing wildly, Rothbart went into his castle. There, he fell silent. "Prince Derek's vow could still break the spell!" he told the hag. "What am I going to do?"

He looked at the old, ugly woman and had an idea. "I know! I'll get Derek to offer his vow to the wrong princess. Don't you see? I'll make you look like Odette."

Rothbart rubbed his hands together gleefully. It would be Odette's ruin. It would be perfect.

That night, under a moonless sky, Rothbart locked Odette in the water dungeon.

"Too bad you can't go to the ball," he taunted her from a window high above. "But I can bring the ball to you. The prince is busy, of course. But here is a substitute. This scared little fellow got lost in the woods."

The hag shoved Bromley down into the dungeon. "Help! Help!" Bromley cried, splashing around the water. "I can't swim!"

Odette dragged him to safety, just as Rothbart slammed the window shut.

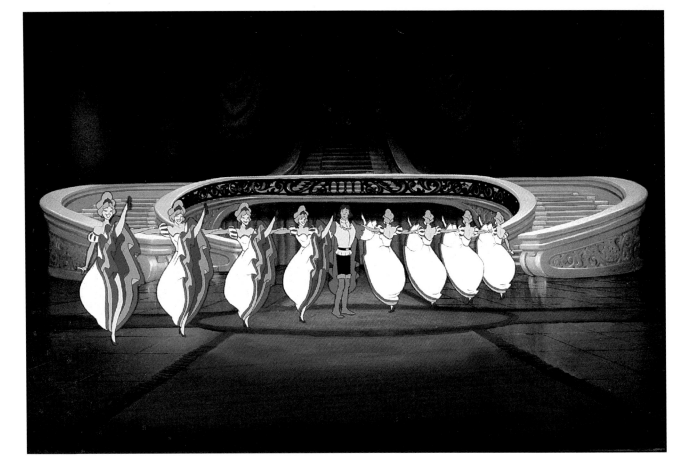

At the castle, the ball was already underway. The prince was growing anxious. Odette had still not arrived. Though he was surrounded by pretty princesses, Derek could think of no one else. Had something gone wrong? Was Odette in trouble? Then there was a loud knock. Slowly, the castle door swung open. A woman walked inside.

"It can't be!" whispered Queen Uberta.

But it was. The woman was Odette . . . or so the prince believed.

The real Odette was still a prisoner in the water dungeon. Luckily, Puffin had another idea: Jean-Bob and Speed would save her! Jean-Bob dove to the watery depths of the moat, searching for a hole in the dungeon wall. At last, he found one. He squeezed inside and dug at the wall, while Speed — faster than any turtle had ever moved before — was digging on the outside. Soon there was a hole large enough for Odette and Bromley to fit through.

"To the rescue, Mademoiselle," said Jean-Bob, bowing low. Bromley, though, was too scared to move. And Odette didn't have a second to waste. She shot through the opening, up through the water, and into the sky.

Meanwhile, the prince was at the ball, dancing with the wrong Odette. "Something about you seems different," he said to her, sounding worried. The hag said nothing. She just showed him the locket — the same locket he had given Odette when she was a baby. Derek smiled, feeling better. She was still the same Odette, after all. "I have an announcement to make," he said loudly, facing everyone in the room. It was time to make his vow of love.

The real Odette was streaking through the sky. She was getting closer. But she was still nowhere in sight.

Finally Odette reached the castle. Flapping her wings, she hovered close to a window. Inside, she saw Derek grasp the hag's hand.

"Today," he was saying, "I have found my bride."

Using all her strength, Odette beat the window with her wings. "It's a trick!" she shouted.

Derek didn't hear. "And now before the world," he continued, "I make a vow. A vow stronger than all the powers on earth. A vow of everlasting love. . . ."

Odette fell silent. She just stared in horror as the prince said, ". . . A vow to Odette."

Suddenly the ballroom windows flew open. A cold wind rushed in. And there, in all his frightening glory, stood Rothbart.

"You've pledged your love to another," he told Prince Derek. "Not to Odette." With that, he sent a spray of mist over the hag. Crumpling into a heap, the hag fell to the ground. And when she raised her head, she was old and ugly once again.

"Now Odette is doomed!" Rothbart roared, pointing out the window.

At last Derek saw the real Odette, flying weakly away.

Derek ran out of the castle. He jumped on horseback, then raced deep into the forest. "Odette!" he called. "Odette!"

Above the trees, Odette was struggling to reach Swan Lake. With her last ounce of strength, she dipped among the leaves, until finally she sank onto the stones by Rothbart's castle.

Speed, Puffin, and Jean-Bob gathered around. "Please, Odette. Don't die!" cried Jean-Bob. All of a sudden, the swan was surrounded by a brilliant light. When it faded away, Princess Odette was lying motionless on the ground.

Just then Derek came crashing through the trees, rushing to Odette's side. "It's you I love," he said. "The vow I made was for you!"

Derek whirled around as Rothbart magically appeared. "Don't you dare let her die!" Derek shouted. "You have the power. Save her!"

"Only if you defeat me!" Rothbart said, turning into the Great Animal. He spread his enormous wings and opened his beak, screeching.

Derek and the Great Animal faced each other, ready for battle. "Get the prince's bow — the one Rothbart threw into the lake," Puffin whispered to Speed and Jean-Bob.

The turtle and the frog dove to the lake bottom, and pulled out the bow from a tangle of weeds. Quickly, they tossed it to the prince. Now Derek held the bow, but there was still a problem. He didn't have any arrows. And the Great Animal was closing in.

"Oh please, oh please, oh please," cried a familiar-sounding voice.

"Bromley?" the prince said, confused. "Is that you?"

Having escaped from the water dungeon, Bromley released an arrow. Just as he had done in Catch and Fire practice earlier, he was aiming the arrow straight for Prince Derek's heart. Derek caught it, then spun around, fitting it into his bow. A second later, he sent the arrow flying. *Pffft*! It struck the Great Animal, and he fell into the lake.

31

Derek hurried to Odette, then cradled her in his arms. "Forgive me," he said. "I only wanted to prove my love."

Slowly, Odette began to stir. Then she opened her eyes. "Oh, Derek!" she whispered, already growing stronger.

Derek had made his vow of everlasting love.

The two embraced, happily reunited, happily in love. And that's the way it would be on their wedding day and forever after.